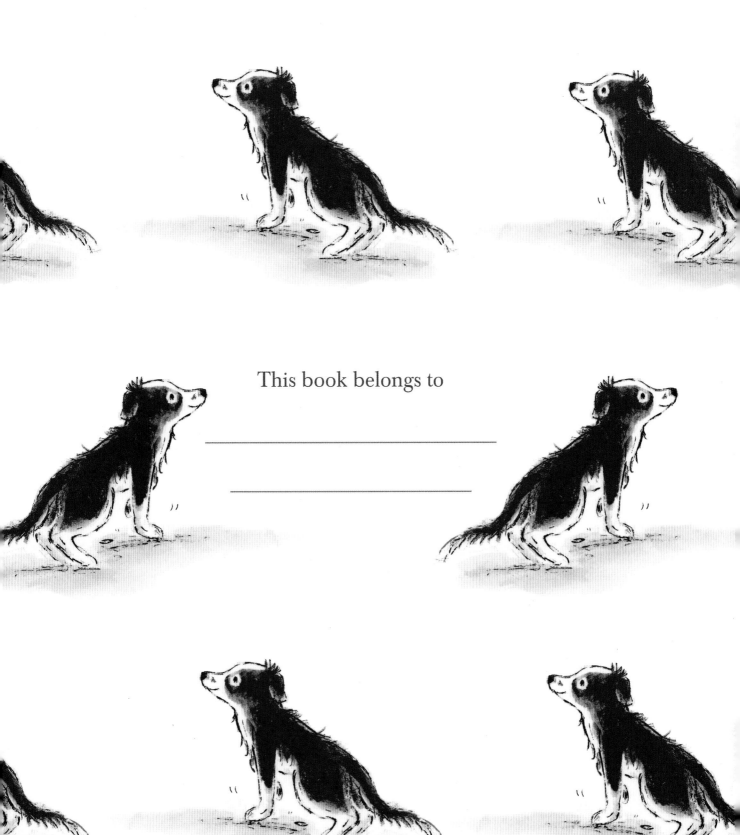

This book belongs to

_____

_____

For Peg, Donald, Senna and Caj

Picture Kelpies is an imprint of Floris Books. First published in 2015 by Floris Books. Text and illustrations © 2015 Sandra Klaassen
Sandra Klaassen has asserted her right under the Copyright, Designs and Patent Act 1988 to be identified as the Author and Illustrator of this
Work. All rights reserved. No part of this publication may be reproduced without prior permission of Floris Books, 15 Harrison Gardens,
Edinburgh www.florisbooks.co.uk. The publisher acknowledges subsidy from Creative Scotland towards the publication of this volume
British Library CIP Data available. ISBN 978-178250-181-7 Printed in Malaysia

Peg
the
Little Sheepdog

Sandra Klaassen

Floris Books

Once there was a beautiful, grassy Scottish island.

Many sheep lived on this island.
They were looked after by sheepdogs like Kim.

Kim belonged to a crofter, who had trained her when she was young. She worked hard gathering his sheep.

One spring, Kim had six puppies.
They slept in a bed of straw to keep warm.

They grew quickly, and were bold
and busy, except for the smallest one,
who preferred hiding.
Her name was Peg.

When Kim wasn't working she took her pups outside.
They liked playing and helping to look after the sheep.

Except for Peg – she was too shy.
She was even frightened of lambs.

As the puppies grew big enough, they were chosen one by one to be sheepdogs for other crofters. Except for Peg.

No crofter wanted a sheepdog who was scared of sheep.

Peg's brothers and sisters were gone. She was growing up.
She wasn't a little puppy any more, but she was still shy.

Her mum, Kim, was in the fields all day, working.
Peg was often on her own, and she was lonely.

Then, one day, we moved in nearby. We wanted Peg from the moment we saw her.

So she came to live with us.

As long as we were close by, Peg was happy to play.

Because she was shy, Peg hadn't been a good working dog. But she also found it hard to be a good family dog.

She hid when we played music.

She whimpered at night when we went to bed
and she was left on her own.

She was nervous of a little lamb who was staying in our
neighbour's field.

And because she had grown up outside on the croft, Peg didn't know how to live in a house.

She thought the sofa was especially for her.

She didn't know that she should only eat food
from her own dish.

She didn't want to come back home when
we were out for a walk.

So we made a plan.

We encouraged Peg to be less shy.

And gave her treats when she obeyed our calls.

We had clear rules about the sofa, the table and the kitchen.

And we moved her bed into the hall, closer to our bedrooms, so she would feel better about being alone at night.

Most importantly, we gave her loads and loads and loads of cuddles so she felt safer and stronger.

Bit by bit, Peg, the sheepdog who was afraid of sheep, became less shy…

...and sometimes even a bit brave.

We were so proud of her.